JOEY PANDA
AND HIS FOOD ALLERGIES SAVE THE DAY

by Amishi S. Murthy, MD and Vivian Chou, MD
illustrated by Joseph Cannon

ISBN-13 - 978-0615668420

ISBN-10 - 0615668429

The information in this book is intended to provide informative material on the subject addressed. It is not intended to replace professional medical advice. Any use of the information in this book is solely at the reader's discretion. The author and publisher specifically disclaim any and all liability, arising directly or indirectly from the use or application of any information in the book. A healthcare professional should always be consulted regarding your specific situation.

First published 2013 by Chicago Allergist Publications

Note from the Authors

As allergists, we are concerned about the rising incidence of food allergy and the increased risk factors for fatality among children with food allergies, namely: lack of self-injectable epinephrine on hand, having a peanut allergy, being a teenager, and having asthma. Nearly two-hundred people die a year due to food allergies and many of these fatalities are preventable.

Like many of our patients, our hero Joey Panda has multiple food allergies. As physicians, we are often privy to the anxiety both children and parents face when dealing with food allergies at school, at lunch, or at the playground. Most children grow up to be teenagers who, naturally, want to fit in with their peers. Some may not want to carry epinephrine because they don't want to feel "different." We want to instill in our patients, during their most formative years, the importance of carrying epinephrine at all times. Through Joey, we hope to convey to our young readers that they may enjoy a relatively normal lifestyle, as long as they are vigilant about their food allergies.

Our hope is that by educating children at a young age, we can empower them with the self-confidence and knowledge to <u>always</u> carry epinephrine and <u>always</u> ask about allergens in food, and perhaps prevent fatal outcomes from food allergy. We ultimately hope to instill in the child the confidence to carry a life-saving epinephrine injector at all times.

ASMurthymD

VChou mD

Amishi Murthy, MD   Vivian Chou, MD

Joey Panda was getting ready for bed, and he was feeling scared about school the next day.

"Are you excited to start first grade?" asked Mama Panda.

"I am really scared, Mommy." said Joey. "I have so many food allergies — peanut, tree nut, egg, milk, soy, wheat, fish, and shellfish. What if all of the kids make fun of me?"

"Oh, Joey," Mama Panda said, and hugged Joey tightly. "People will love you because you are funny and kind and smart."

Mama Panda kissed Joey good night. But Joey was still worried, and he had trouble going to sleep.

That night, Joey had scary dreams about his first day of school.

The next morning, he ate his breakfast quietly.

"How is my big first-grader doing today?" asked Papa Panda.

"I am still a little scared," said Joey.

"You will do great in school, Joey. Do you remember what to ask before eating anything?"

Joey said, "Does this food have peanut, tree nut, egg, milk, soy, wheat, fish, or shellfish? If it does, I cannot eat it, because it will make me VERY sick."

"And what do you always have with you?"

"Eppy," replied Joey.

Eppy was a medicine that went everywhere with Joey – to school, to the playground, and to friends' houses.

If Joey ate something he wasn't supposed to, a grown-up could give him Eppy.

Eppy could save his life.

It was VERY important that Eppy went EVERYWHERE with Joey. Joey felt safer with Eppy around.

"Have a great first day of school, Joey!" Mama Panda hugged Joey tightly.

At school, Joey
walked around
by himself.

Joey felt a tap on his shoulder. "Hi, my name is Chris Frog. What's your name?"

Joey looked up. "I'm Joey Panda."

"Do you want to play?" asked Chris.

"Uh, okay," said Joey. "But I have to tell you, I have many food allergies. I can get really, really sick."

"Oh, I know all about food allergies," said Chris. "My big brother has a bad allergy to peanut. He brings his Eppy wherever he goes."

"He does?" said Joey. "Does he have friends?"

"Of course, he has lots of friends!" said Chris. "Let's go! I think we're in Mr. Elephant's class together."

"Hmm," Joey thought, "maybe I can have food allergies AND still have friends."

Joey loved Mr. Elephant's class. They all played games and laughed a lot!

"Okay, class," said Mr. Elephant. "We are going to do an exciting project today. We are going to build tree houses using macaroni noodles, frosting, and gingerbread!"

"Uh-oh," thought Joey. "I don't think I'm supposed to touch those foods."

"Uh, excuse me, Mr. Elephant?" said Joey. "I have lots of food allergies. I don't think that I can do this project."

"Joey, you are right," said Mr. Elephant.

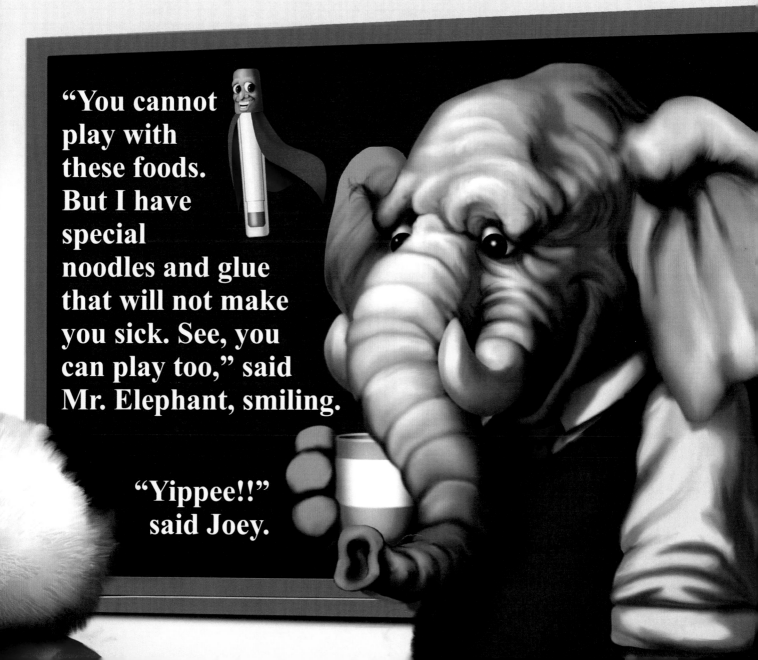

"You cannot play with these foods. But I have special noodles and glue that will not make you sick. See, you can play too," said Mr. Elephant, smiling.

"Yippee!!" said Joey.

"Ooh, I like your project. What's your name?" said Siena Rabbit.

"I'm Joey Panda. What's yours?"

"I'm Siena Rabbit. Let's be friends."

"Okay!"

Lunchtime came, and Joey was excited to sit with his new friends. He was also scared about being around food that could make him sick.

"Hi," said Joey, feeling braver now.
"My name is Joey Panda. What's yours?"

"Hi! I'm Lily Peacock. Do you want some of my sandwich?"

"No, thanks. I am allergic to peanut, tree nut, egg, milk, soy, wheat, fish, and shellfish. I can't share other people's food, because it might have something in it that could make me sick."

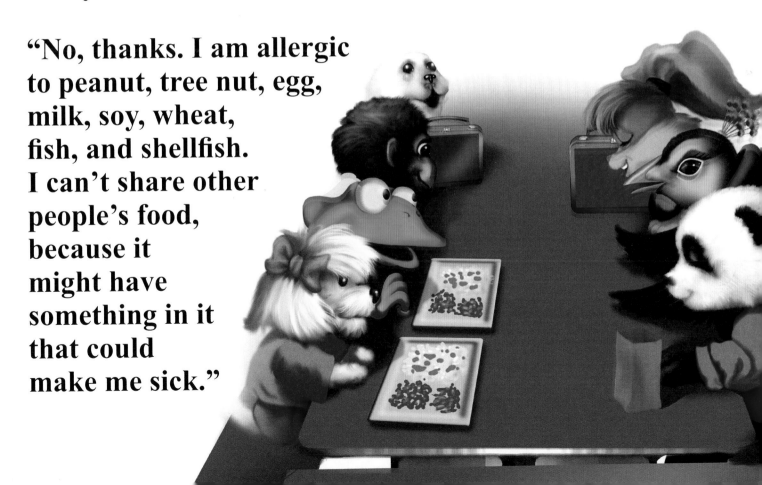

"Really?" Lily's eyes grew bigger. "This sandwich could make you sick?"

"Yup," said Joey. "REALLY sick."

"I didn't know that! But we can be friends, right?"

"I think so!" said Joey.

"Hmm, that wasn't too bad," thought Joey. "As long as I tell everyone that I have food allergies, I can stay healthy."

Recess was so much fun!
Joey was climbing the tree house...

...when he saw Kevin Lion
eat a cookie.

Suddenly, Kevin's lips started to get bigger, and he got red bumps all over his body.

"I think Kevin might be getting sick from something he ate," thought Joey. "That happened to me when I ate a peanut."

Joey ran to Kevin. "Kevin, I think something in the cookie is making you sick. We need to see the school nurse right now."

"I don't feel so good," said Kevin. He started to cough and looked scared.

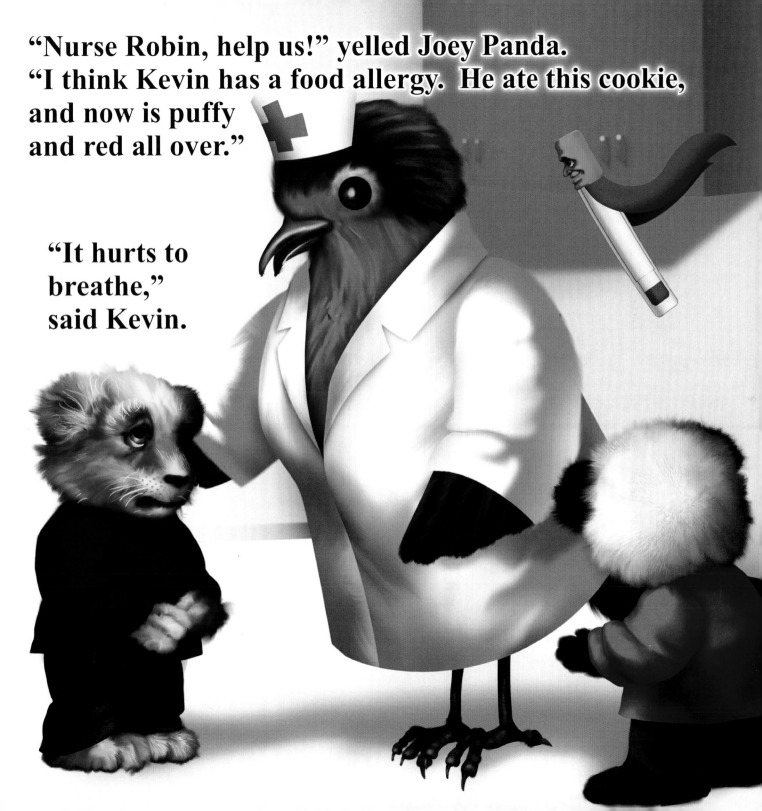

"Nurse Robin, help us!" yelled Joey Panda. "I think Kevin has a food allergy. He ate this cookie, and now is puffy and red all over."

"It hurts to breathe," said Kevin.

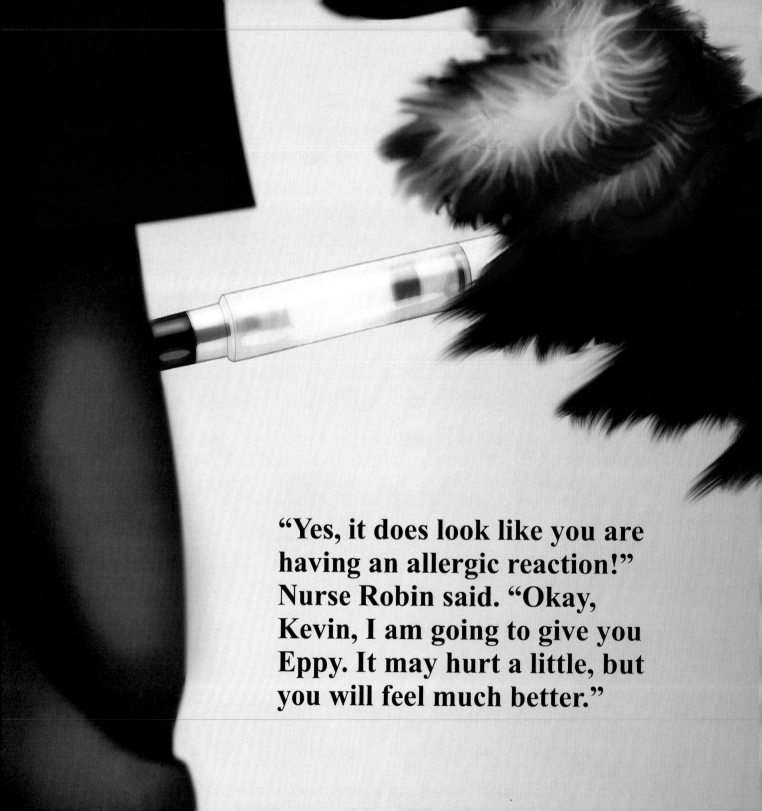

"Yes, it does look like you are having an allergic reaction!" Nurse Robin said. "Okay, Kevin, I am going to give you Eppy. It may hurt a little, but you will feel much better."

A few minutes after getting Eppy, Kevin said, "Oh, I feel a lot better, Nurse Robin. My throat doesn't feel funny anymore. Can I go play now?"

"NO!" said Joey and Nurse Robin together. "You have to go to the hospital, where a doctor will look at you and make sure you are okay."

The ambulance came
and took Kevin to the hospital.

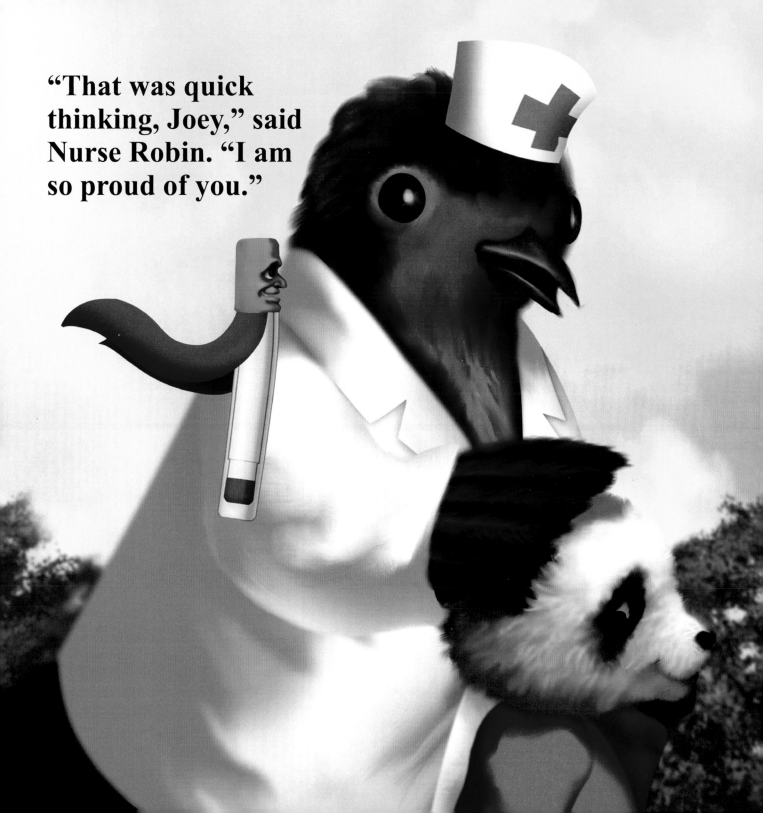

"That was quick thinking, Joey," said Nurse Robin. "I am so proud of you."

"I am so glad that you knew what to do, Joey," said Chris. "That was so scary."

"Yay for Joey! Yay for Joey!" shouted the other kids.

That night, as Mama Panda tucked Joey into bed, she asked, "So how was your first day of school?"

"Oh, Mommy, it was great. I made so many friends. But it was also scary."

Joey told his mom about his day.

"But I think I'm really going to like first grade."

"As long as I have Eppy with me, and I tell everyone I have an allergy to peanut, tree nut, egg, milk, soy, wheat, fish and shellfish, I can have friends and be like everyone else."

"Well, I don't know if you will be like EVERYONE else, Joey," said Mama Panda.

"Why not?" asked Joey, looking scared again.

"Because you are MY Joey and you are the most special person to me!" Mama Panda said as they laughed and she kissed Joey good night.

CPSIA information can be obtained
at www.ICGtesting.com
Printed in the USA
LVXC02n1106111113
360831LV00001B/4